Whispers in the Dark

WHISPERS IN THE DARK

THREE STORIES OF TERROR

N. J. HANSON

Ink Drop Press
Chico, CA

Contents:

Inked In Blood

Chapter 1: The Pen

"You have deadlines to meet!" My agent shouted at me over the phone. "I don't have to remind you of that disaster you wrote last time. If you don't have something reasonable to go to the proofs by this Friday, then you're off the project! Do you get it?"

"Yes, I understand." I let out an exasperated sigh.

"Then what are you doing? Get back to work and give me something readable!" The line went dead as he hung up.

I set my phone on the desk next to my keyboard

and folded my arms. I stared at the computer screen, a prompt flashed in an open word doc. There were no words in the document. I hadn't written anything in days, and I was beginning to go crazy from it.

A stack of open letters and envelopes sat next to my laptop. There were fan letters, although "hate mail" was a better description. Not a single positive thing to say among them, I guess that's what happens when you try to write outside your fan base's comfort zone. And these were just the physical letters sent to the publishing house; they didn't include the gigabytes of rage and rants online.

The problem was that I tried to branch out and try something new. As a primarily horror writer, I wanted to try my hand at a different genre and wrote a melodramatic romance. I thought it was good, but everyone else tore it to shreds.

Now, however, I have a chance at redemption. This short fiction horror anthology goes to the proofreaders on Friday, and my story is supposed to be the main headliner, but I've had nothing to write this entire past week. For once in my life, the well of ideas I usually draw from has gone dry. On top of that, my backlog of works I'd normally have stored away just in case of such an event was also empty.

I got up and paced around my office. It was Tuesday, about four o'clock in the afternoon, and the only light in the room illuminating it from the computer screen. Nothing. I had no ideas, nothing to write. Writer's block always strikes at the most inopportune times.

Something brushed up against my leg and I stopped pacing. Salem, my green-eyed black cat, pressed his face against my ankles before looking up at me. He purred and flicked his tail.

"Yeah, I know." I picked him up and cradled him in the crook of my arm. "You're hungry, you greedy thing." He meowed a response. I carried him back to the kitchen where I opened a can of tuna for him. He licked and nibbled at it hungrily.

Leaving the cat in the kitchen, I grabbed my coat and headed out the door. I needed inspiration. And when I need inspiration, I usually go on a small window-shopping spree.

The small town flea market was my destination

today. I paid my two bucks to get in and began browsing up and down the booths and tables. Flea markets were my usual choice for inspiring ideas, as the items there are often unique and have some kind of story behind them. Today, however, there was little of interest. There was one booth with a man trying to sell his old collection of baseball cards, another table with a huge selection of old VHS tapes, and one man with a bunch of garden tools. Of the three, the garden tools looked the most likely to give me some kind of inspiration, but even that wasn't doing anything for me. It was really a slow day at the flea market.

At the very end of the hall, however, there sat a fourth table. As I approached, I found it was covered in row after row of hard cover books, most of which were written by authors who never got a second book deal or even a second printing. But as I walked past, I noticed a disproportionate number of them had been written by one author in particular: Harry Warcroft.

Harry Warcroft was once a giant of the horror writing world. His books had sold in the millions and had been adapted into dozens of record-breaking films. Some of his fans used to call him the second coming of H. P. Lovecraft. It was a shock to the horror community when he died.

I stopped by this table and ran my fingers over the spines of the books. A lot of these were first editions and all of them were hardcover. This piqued my interest, as I prefer hardbacks to paperbacks any day.

"I see you have good taste in literature, my friend," the vendor said. He sat on a folding metal chair against the wall behind the table. He had slick black hair and piercing blue eyes with a smirk across his face. His arms were folded over his chest and legs crossed. "A fan of the late Warcroft?"

"Yeah, I've read most of these already," I said. I picked up one of the Harry Warcroft books and turned it over in my hands. His name was printed in red, bold-faced letters that took up the top third of the front cover. The title, *The Haunting of Raven's Peak,* was printed in smaller letters along the lower fourth of the book. Between the author's name and the title was a small picture of a decrepit mountain village falling to ruin. This one I'd never read before, and for good reason; it was supposedly a lost book. "How did you get this one?"

"Aw, I see you've found the crown piece of my collection." The vendor stood and approached me. He twirled a scarlet red fountain pen in his fingers. "I got that on its release night. I stood in line outside the bookstore for three hours waiting to get that. Did you know there were only ever 10,000 copies printed?"

"Yes. I preordered mine online, but then Warcroft bought the publication rights back from the agency and swore to never let this book be published again," I said. I flipped the cover open and found Harry Warcroft's name scrawled across the title page in red fountain ink. "And an autographed copy at that. You must have sold your soul to get this thing."

The man let out a soft chuckle. "Not quite. But it was an amazing experience getting to meet him. As a matter of fact, this was the pen he autographed it with." He held up the fountain pen and twirled it between his fingers.

My eyebrows arched and I nodded. "That's pretty amazing."

"I know, right?" The vendor let out another small chuckle. "Being such a fan of his work, I'm sure you know the story behind it, right?"

"You mean his inspiration?" I asked.

"Not exactly. More like the actual writing itself." The vendor placed his hands against the table and leaned forward. "They say that when he wrote the book, he did it longhand with a fountain pen. But the story was too frightening, even for him. It steadily drove him mad to keep writing it, but he felt compelled to do so. He couldn't leave the house, couldn't do anything, not even sleep until that book was done. Eventually, he started to run out of ink. Desperate to finish the book, Warcroft started mixing the remaining ink with his own blood and using that to write. Soon the last of the ink ran out and the book was completed using only his blood." He pushed himself back up. "It's probably not true, but it makes for a good story."

I stared down at the book in my hands. "I have to admit, that's pretty creepy. Especially considering what happened to him later."

"Oh, yeah. Can't forget about that." The vendor said. "It was his house maid who found him, right?"

"The day after he bought the rights to this book back." I replied. "He'd slit his wrists in the bathtub, bleed out overnight. Such a tragedy." While I was amazed to find such a treasure, I tried not to outwardly show it. "So since this thing is so rare, why are you trying to sell it in the first place?"

"I need the money. A valuable book doesn't do anyone any good sitting on a bookshelf collecting dust." He said, motioning with the pen.

"But still, why at a flea market? Why not put it up on eBay or something like that?"

"I don't trust any of those online dealers. I'd much rather speak with the buyer face to face." The vendor said. He pointed at the book with the pen. "You seem rather interested, though."

"Oh, yes. Very." I ran my hands over the front

cover, feeling the raised letters of the title and author's name. "How much were you hoping to sell it for?"

"Well, that's always the question, isn't it?" He twirled the pen in his fingers before setting it down on the table. "How about… what's it worth to you?"

"I see. Put me on the spot." I held the book out at arms length and inspected it. The cover and dust jacket were both in perfect condition, the inside pages were clean and with no signs of wear or tear, and it even had the author's signature on the title page. "It's in such good condition; I'd almost give this the list price."

"Well, if I put it at that, then I'd never sell it. How about $10?" The vendor asked.

I gave a shrug. "I can do that." I pulled out my wallet and handed him a ten dollar bill.

"Alright, thank your for your business." He said as he took my money.

"And thank you." I tucked the book up under my arm and left the flea market. Only once I was back in the car and half way home did I realize I forgot the entire reason I'd gone there in the first place. I still had no inspiration of what to write.

Once I got back home, I placed the book on my desk and went back to my computer. The prompt was still flashing on the blank word document screen. Sitting in the chair, staring at the computer, I gave a heavy sigh and thrust my hands into my pockets.

I felt a long, cold, cylindrical shape in my coat

pocket. I pulled it out. Looking down at my hand, I found myself holding a red fountain pen. For a moment, I was confused as to where this had come from, but then I realized this was the flea market vendor's pen. I must have grabbed it subconsciously when I was leaving.

As I twirled it around in my fingers, an idea came to me. Not necessarily a story idea, but more of how to write the story. I closed my laptop, pulled open the side drawer of my desk, and grabbed a spiral notebook and a bottle of fountain ink. I filled the pen, then left my office and moved to the living room. With my window open to let in air and sunlight, I sat down on the couch and held the tip of the pen to the page.

And it was in that moment that an idea popped

into my head, one that I knew would be perfect for the horror anthology. A tale of a man who moves into a new house, one he gets for a very reasonable price, which is also haunted by the spirits of the family that was murdered there.

Chapter 2: The Story

The rusty old hinges protested loudly as Thomas pushed the door open. The lock was so old he'd been afraid the key would break when he tried to turn it. Now, stepping inside, he saw the reason why the price was so low. A thick layer of dust had settled over everything, cobwebs reached between every nook and cranny in the house. While the front of the house looked okay, the inside appeared to be in extreme neglect. If he hadn't been so desperate to move in, he likely would have taken the offer to at least look it over before buying, and never bought the house.

It was all a moot point now. The moving truck would be here any minute. Thomas stepped inside and made his way around the house. There was a short hallway leading to a staircase and the three bedrooms and single bathroom on the second floor. A kitchen and living room conjoined near the front door, and a two-car garage set off to the side of the house. He already was making plans on what to do with the other bedrooms, settling on the idea of a study room and a small library, when the sound of a large truck engine alerted him to the movers.

I wrote in this fashion for several hours, my hand cramped occasionally and forced me to stop for a few minutes before I could take up the pen again and write some more. The words just flowed from my mind like water over a cliff, running down my arm to my fingertips and onto the page. I had to stop at least once to refill the pen as the ink ran out. When I did, I remembered what the vendor had said about Warcroft, about him using his own blood to fill the pen and write. I gave a small chuckle at the thought. Fortunately, I had enough ink, so I wouldn't have to do the same thing.

Eventually the light became so dim I had to get

up and turn on the ceiling lamp to continue. Once I did that, I realized just how long I must have been sitting there. In the middle of April, the sun usually doesn't go down until around seven thirty, so it must've been well after that. Probably closer to eight. I'd gone to the flea market around four and was home by five, meaning I've been writing for almost three hours straight. That's the longest I've ever spent in a single writing session, and especially without breaks.

I picked up the notebook and flipped through what I'd already written. I like it so far, as most writers do after scribbling a few lines on the page. What I needed to do now was take a break and come back to it later. I set my notebook back down on the living room coffee table and retreated to my bedroom. My eyes hurt, my hand still ached, and I felt exhausted. A lot of non-writers don't seem to realize just how tiring it can be to write nonstop for hours at a time. Even I get surprised by it sometimes.

In my bedroom I stripped off my clothes and put on sleepwear. Even though I live alone with just a cat and write short stories to make ends meet, I still try to give myself an air of sophistication, even if it's just for my own sake. I climbed into bed, rested on top of the blankets, and turned on the TV. The show didn't even reach its first commercial break when I heard a loud crash coming from the kitchen. It made me jump and my heart skip a beat.

Slowly, I crawled off my bed and fell to my knees. In my bedside mantle I kept my revolver and several rounds of ammunition. I bought it in response to all the hate mail and death threats I'd gotten recently. I loaded the gun, stood up, and moved down the hall back to the living room.

I held the revolver out in front of me, pointing it at every shadow that moved. I turned on every light as I went and left them on. Stepping back into the kitchen I discovered the source of the crash. The flower vase, the one I usually have sitting on the counter, had fallen to the floor. Its shattered remains littered the linoleum, which was now covered with water and flowers. My cat, Salem, stood on the counter where the vase used to be. His back was hunched and tail perked up. Must've startled the hell out of himself when he knocked it down.

"Salem." I said with a sigh. "Look what you did. That was my nice vase." I lowered my gun for the first time since picking it up.

He looked up at me with his big green eyes, his haunches fell back to the counter top and he sat down, looking confident in himself now. He tilted his head and gave a soft mew in response.

"Is that all you can say for yourself?" I grabbed the broom and dustpan to pick up the remains of the vase and flowers before getting the mop out of the closet to clean up the water. The whole time Salem just sat, stared at me, and occasionally lick his paws. With all that done, I put everything away and came back to my cat. He was still on the counter, grooming himself. "You've a sassy little twerp, aren't you?" He didn't even look up at me for that one. I picked him up and scratched him behind the ears. He purred, his face nuzzled against my hand. "Come on, dumb cat. Time for bed."

The next morning I awoke and immediately went back to writing. At first I took what was in the notebook and typed it into the word document, but when I tried to continue on the computer the ideas just didn't come to me. I stared at the screen blankly, trying to remember where I wanted the story to go. Eventually I turned off my computer in frustration. As I stormed around my office angrily, I spotted the notebook and the fountain pen right next to the keyboard. With a shrug I picked them back up and moved into the living room. Once I was on the couch, pen pressed to the page, the story unfolded in my mind once again.

"Hello?" Thomas called as he moved around the downstairs of his house. The floorboards creaked and moaned as if someone were walking around on them, but there was no one else in the house. At least, there shouldn't be.

The wind howled outside, rain pounded against the windows. Thomas's hand slid along the wall until it came to the light switch. He flicked it up, but nothing happened. Anxiously, he clicked it up and down to no effect. The storm had knocked out the power.

There was a flash of lightning and for an

instant the room was illuminated, then fell into total blackness again. For that brief microsecond of light, Thomas saw another person standing across the room from him. It was a girl, her hair was long, black, and unkempt. Her skin was a stark white, along with the gown she wore which reached all the way down to her ankles. Her face remained hidden in shadow.

A scream caught in Thomas's throat and he jumped back, the wall pressed against him from behind. His breathing became quick and shallow. Had he just seen what he thought he saw? Who was that? What were they doing in his house?

With his back to the wall, he started to creep back down the hallway to the stairs. He grasped the handrail firmly, placed his left foot on the lowest step, and began to climb.

At about two thirds of the way up he was starting to feel a little better. It must've just been the effects of the lightning flash, like an after-image in his mind. He still walked backwards up the stairs however, keeping a watchful eye on the darkness below. He reached the top in safety, took a deep breath, and let it out in relief. Whatever he had seen, it was gone now.

Just as he turned around there was another

strike of lightning. The bright flash shown in from the windows and he saw the figure again. She stood in front of him, closer this time, and between him and the bedroom.

Thomas jumped. His hand grasped the stair railing just as his feet teetered on the of the step. His heart hammered in his chest and his palms were sweaty. It quickly dawned on him that if he hadn't grabbed the railing just now he would have fallen down the stairs and likely died; his neck snapped in two and a dozen other bones shattered along the way.

A faint light shown in from the hall windows,

from which Thomas was able to make out the silhouette of the girl. Her foot, covered in dirt and mud, lifted up an pressed back against the floor as she advanced towards him. Her movements were unnatural, jerky and wild. Her head shifted from one side to the other, bending in awkward angles as she walked. Between the twisting of her neck and the subsequent flipping of her hair, Thomas saw her face. Her eyes were–

The loud ringing of my phone jolted me out of the story. With an irritated groan I set the notebook down and stood up. My phone was back in the office. I made it there just in time to catch the name of the number and answered it. It was my manager again. "Hey, Vic," I said as I picked it up, " how are things?"

"How are things You still haven't given me anything, that's how they are! Please tell me you have something by now!"

"As a matter if fact, I do. I was writing it just as you called. When I finish it, I'll send it your way." I said.

"Well, that's good. Just try to get it done by tonight. The proof's have to look at it on Friday, remember."

"Yes, I haven't forgotten. Now, if you'll excuse me, I have more story to get back to." I pressed the disconnect button and turned my phone off before setting it back down. I didn't want to have any further interruptions. Stepping back into the living room, I found Salem seated on the coffee table. His haunches rested on my notebook as he batted at the pen. I sighed and scratched him behind the ears again. "Come on, silly cat. Need you to move." I picked him up and set him on the couch before gathering my writing utensils again to continue toe story.

-as white as the rest of her skin. Her lips looked like hey had been chewed off, leaving just her black gums and stained teeth behind.

A shiver ran down the length of Thomas's spine. Even behind the rot and disgust, he recognized her. She had been in that newspaper article he found; the one detailing the previous owners of the house. But that article was almost two years old, what was she doing here?

It became obviously clear to him that this was a ghost, her restless spirit come back to haunt the house she was murdered in.

The house rattled, windows shook, and the floorboards creaked in the gale force wind. Rain splattered against the glass and another flash of lightning illuminated the hallway. The ghostly figure moved closer, her milky white eyes fixed upon Thomas. A raspy hiss came from between her teeth. Thomas tried to run, but his legs were frozen in place. Cold sweat ran down his face. His heart raced like he'd never felt it before.

"This is mine." Her voice was low, barely above a whisper and hardly audible over the howling wind. "Get out." She suddenly flew at him with incredible speed, the wispy chill of her ghostly form engulfed him.

Thomas released his grip on the handrail and instinctively threw his arms over his face. The ghost pushed him back, his foot teetered on the edge of the step, he lost his footing, and he fell. He screamed just as the back of his skull smashed against the edge of the step. He tumbled end over end, bones snapped and shattered under his own weight as he rolled back down the stairs. At the very bottom, his head hit the ground at an awkward angle and his neck snapped.

The story went on only a little further after this. I finished it; my hand ached from holding the pen for so long, and set it aside. Leaning back on the couch, I breathed a sigh of relief. It was done. I had something to give my manager.

Salem hopped up on my lap. He tilted his head up at me, his tail flicked back and forth.

"Yeah, I know. You want your tuna, don't you?" I said as I scratched his ears. He rubbed his face against my hand affectionately. Or at least a mockery of affection, who knows how much cats actually care about their owners. "Okay, come on." I picked him up under his torso and carried his back to the kitchen to prepare his mid morning snack.

Later that day I sat down at the computer and typed up everything I wrote. I fixed a few things while I did, some of the plot holes and story issues that became apparent after a second viewing. Once it was done, I saved it and sent it off to my agent.

Chapter 3: The Apparition

The next morning I got a call from the anthology manager. "I have to admit, this is probably the best thing we've gotten out of you." He said. "I'm serious; it almost reads like a piece from that Warcroft guy."

"Coming from you, that's a compliment." I replied.

"And I mean every word of it. This is sure to win back your crowd. Also, thanks for getting this to us on time. I was almost afraid we were going to have to take you off the project. Once it goes to print, we'll be sending your free copies, as usual. Once again, great story." The line went dead as he hung up.

The rest of my day went by calm and smooth. It was a beautiful sunny day, not a cloud in the sky. I decided that since I was no longer under a time crunch, I could take a walk out to the park and read my new book. Something about reading next to a babbling brook with a light breeze in my face has always appealed to me, ever since I was a kid.

I soon found myself sitting on a wooden bench, the trees reaching up from the dirt and gravel of the creek to partially obscure the sunlight, and the wind sweeping by all around me. Bicyclists rode by on the path occasionally, chiming their bells to alert the pedestrians. I took my new book, *The Haunting of Raven's Peak*, out from under my arm and cracked it open. My eyes instantly fell upon the signature written in red ink across the title page.

To own one of the few existing copies of Harry Warcroft's final book filled me with a sense of glee, like what a young baseball fan would feel if the had a ball or bat signed by Babe Ruth himself. And not only that, but to have the very pen used to sign it. I flipped past the title page and began to read.

I don't know how long I sat upon that bench, it must have been hours, but I was fully engrossed in the story up until the moment I heard a distant rumbling. Looking up from my book I saw a dark mass of storm clouds gathering on the horizon. I stood up, placed the dust jacket inside the pages to keep my place, and tucked the book back under my arm. There wasn't any storm warning from the weather report today; this must be some kind of freak storm.

I was in my car and on my way home when the first droplets of rain hit my windshield. The drive home was less than ten minutes, but even so the rain was coming down in sheets by the time I pulled into the driveway.

Once in the house, I shook the water off my coat. A puddle formed around my feet. I kicked off my shoes and set them by the door. My coat went on the rack. The book, somehow through a sheer miracle, has stayed intact. Salem came out to greet me when I came in, but upon seeing me dripping from head to toe, decided I was best avoided. He slinked away as I hung up my jacket.

"Yeah, thanks, cat. Knew I could always count on you to be there for me." I said as I walked through the house in my socks. I went back to me room and disrobed, got myself into a dry set of clothes, then moved back to the living room and continued reading.

The storm raged on outside, rain pelted my windows, lightning flashed, and thunder rumbled. Then, suddenly, the lights went off throughout my house and everything fell dark. I stood up from the couch. The only light left came in through the windows.

"Okay, what is this?" I demanded. I found a packet of matches and lit a few candles, giving me a little extra light. I set my book aside, after all, it's not as if I can read very well by candlelight, and moved to my larger comfortable chair and reclined it back. Salem jumped into my lap again and promptly lay down. I scratched his ears and stroked his fur. "Oh, yeah. Now you want my company. Silly cat." I fell asleep that way.

A few hours later, I awoke to the sound of something smashing down the hall. I jolted out of the chair, waking Salem as well. It was now fully dark, long past sunset, and the power still wasn't restored. Pulling the matchbook from my pocket, I re-lit the candle. With Salem cradled in the crook of my arm and the candle held at arm's length out in front of me, I walked down the hallway in the direction of the crash. The further I got, the more agitated Salem became. His claws dug into my arm and he squirmed anxiously. With ears pressed flat against his head, he hissed and snarled. I had to clutch him tighter just to keep a grip on him. Finally, his claws slashed into my arm and I released my hold on him. "Ow!" I shouted. He leapt away and raced back in the other direction leaving me alone in the darkness.

With the limited candlelight, I inspected the scratches on my arm. Three long, red marks ran from my wrist all the way to my elbow, light droplets of blood oozed out in scattered points along the way. I gave an aggravated sigh.

Before going any further, I went to my bedroom and grabbed the revolver from the bedside drawer. Whoever was in my house now, or whatever it was, their presence scared the hell out of my cat and I had no desire to run into them unarmed. Not that I thought I could aim very well in the dark with only the light of a candle to go by, but it might be enough to scare them off.

With my gun loaded and held tightly in one hand, I grabbed the candle off the nightstand and prepared to head back out in search of the intruder. That's when I saw her. The same ghostly face as the specter in my story. Pale rotten skin, exposed teeth with no lips, long stringy black hair, and milky white eyes. I screamed and jumped back, my legs caught on the sheets and I fell on the bed. The candle slipped from my hand and the flame extinguished as it fell.

The room was completely dark. I couldn't see my own hand in front of my face, and I had no idea what I'd actually seen in that brief moment. I lay on the bed, gasping for air, feeling like my chest might explode from my racing heart.

There was a raspy hissing sound, like a breath being drawn in. "Get out," A low voice said.

It was her, it must have been, but that was impossible. She was just a figment, a spook from a short story, nothing more. Never the less, I called back to her. "Who… who are you? What do you want?" My voice was weak, like the sound of a weeping child.

"Leave. Never return." The ghost's voice came again.

I sat up on the bed, bracing myself with my arms. "You're the girl, aren't you? The one from my story. You can't be real."

"I'm as real as anything." Her whispering voice

49

echoed throughout the room, coming from all directions. "Leave."

"I won't leave." A renewed sense of bravery filled me. She wasn't real, after all. She was just some figure from a story, brought on by a storm and power outage, that was all. I had no reason to be afraid. "This is my house, not yours."

Something crashed in the room. The television was thrown off its mount and smashed against the wall where it shattered. Sparks flew from the broken components inside. "Get out!" She screamed now. The house rattled. Lightning flashed through the window, followed by the rumble of thunder. In that brief moment, I saw her standing at the foot of my bed, grimacing as much as she could.

Whatever courage I'd gathered up before was rendered moot now. I moved as fast as I could to the wall and followed it to the door. I stumbled in the dark down the hallway, the house still engrossed in darkness. I didn't know where I was anymore, every corner I turned left me further confused. This was my house, but I was so terrified I lost all bearings as to where I was, or where I was supposed to be going.

Lightning streaked across the sky again and the house was illuminated. I found myself standing in the living room at the edge of the kitchen. And once again, standing in front of me, was the ghost girl. She reached out for me with her ragged, dirt-encrusted fingernails about to choke me. I turned to run, but my feet caught on something on the floor.

There was a loud yowling and a flurry of fur and claws as Salem jumped up from under me, his claws tore into my ankles. I stumbled over him, my balance lost. I waved my arms around in the air, but to no avail. The last thing I saw as I fell was the edge of the counter right in front of my face before it collided with my skull.

I lay on the floor as blood poured out from the crater in my head. I couldn't move my arms or legs no matter how I tried. I sputtered for breath, but breathing was nearly impossible. I felt a heavy weight on my chest as Salem sat himself on me. The cat leaned forward and his rough tongue licked up the blood that trickled down my face. My mind was racing now, even as I lay dying. This was it, it was over now.

The ghost girl came to hover over me, causing Salem to hiss and race away. There was something she held between her fingers. She dropped it on my chest. It was the pen, the red fountain pen; the one I got from the vendor, and the same one I used to write her story with.

A pair of orderlies carried Thomas William's body away in a body bag on a stretcher. They loaded him into the ambulance - not that it would do any good - and had him ready to ship off to the morgue. It was the real estate agent, Mr. Ernest Hamilton, who found him the morning after the storm when he came over for a routine check in. He used his personal key to get inside when no one came to the door, and upon finding the broken body of Thomas, immediately called the police. Now, an officer was asking him questions.

"As I told you before, I came by to speak with him about finalizing the agreement for the house and found his body at the base of the stairs." Hamilton said, growing more frustrated as the questions continued.

"And about what time was this?" The officer asked.

"Just after eight. I called you guys as soon as I found him, you can check the records."

The officer placed his hands on his hips and gazed down at the base of the stairs. A red stain had soaked into the hardwood from Thomas's blood. His eyes scanned up the stairs to the top and back down. "Alright," the office finally said, "we have your testimony, and will get an official word from the medical examiner once the autopsy is done. Most likely, he was startled my lightning during the storm last night and slipped. Best I can figure, anyways." He sauntered away from the steps and passed by Mr. Hamilton on his way to the door. "Once all the evidence has been collected and cataloged we'll be out of your hair. And what do you plan to do with the house when that's done?"

Hamilton let out a heavy sigh and shook his head. He pulled off his glasses, rubbed his eyes, and put them back on. "I suppose it'll just go back on the market. Though I don't know who'd be interested in buying it now."

Roadside

With a heave and a groan, he threw the body off the bridge and watched it splash into the river below. The concrete cinder block tied to it quickly pulled the corpse down to the bottom, where the dead girl's arms, legs, and hair listed almost delicately in the current.

He didn't know what would happen now; would her body be eaten by the fish, or would someone find her in the morning and alert the authorities? That wasn't his concern anymore, he was through with her. The man got back into his truck, the old engine of his '73 Chevy rumbled to life when he turned the key, threw it in gear, and drove away. It was time to find a new girl.

* * *

With her arm extended and thumb pointed up, young hitch-hiker Amanda Collins staggered along the side of the high-way, her shoulder bag digging into her arm. The sun had slowly dipped behind the mountains to her left, finally granting her some reprieve from the blistering heat of the Arizona desert. Her feet throbbed with every step she took; she must've walked ten miles so far.

Her hair, soaked with sweat, clung to her face

and neck like wet paper. The grime and grit of the desert sand mixed with the sweat. Every time the wind blew, more dirt collected on her skin and caught in her eyes.

The rumble of an engine alerted her to an oncoming car. Amanda reached her arm out as it approached, but it drove right past and continued on its way. The tenth car today to pass her by, she was keeping track.

Not much later another car appeared, an old rickety pick-up truck with rusted fenders and chipping paint. One of the headlights was busted, and there was a crack in the windshield. This time, the vehicle slowed and came to a stop right behind her.

The driver leaned out his window and waved.

He was an older man, probably mid-forties, with a cowboy hat, blue jeans, a red checkered shirt and boots. "You need a lift, young lady?"

A weight immediately lifted from Amanda's shoulders. She hiked up her shoulder bag and approached the truck. "Yes, thank you, sir," she gasped out of breath. "Can you get me to the next town? I feel like I've been walking for hours."

"Sure." The man gestured his thumb to the passenger door. "Hop in."

Amanda pressed the button on the side door handle and it creaked open. She tossed her bag inside before climbing onto the passenger seat and closing the door behind her. She reclined back in the seat, her head rested against the back window, and he let out a sigh of relief. "Ah, you don't know how nice this is. Just to give my feet a rest for a while."

"I can imagine," the man said. He resettled himself and started the truck again. The engine rumbled and gears ground together as he grabbed the stick and shifted. "This thing doesn't have air conditioning, so don't ask."

"That's fine." Amanda replied, rolling her head from side to side. "Just to get off the road and out of the sun is enough."

The truck started down the road again. Amanda grabbed the window crank and rolled her window down, letting a stream of air blast her in the face. Her hair whipped around in the breeze. "I didn't get your name, mister."

"Call me Frank," he said as he shifted gears.

"Thanks again, Frank. My name's Amanda."

"You're welcome," Frank said. "What are you doing all the way out here anyways? It's at least another fifty miles to the nearest town the way you were going, and more than twenty out from the last one. How'd you get so far in the middle of nowhere?"

"My car broke down," she said. "I think it overheated or something. Steam was just spraying out from the hood, and it wouldn't start again. My phone wouldn't get any service out here, so I just had to start walking."

"Then it's a good thing I found you when I did. You wouldn't have made it to the next town in this heat," Frank said.

While she rested, her head reclined all the way

back and her eyes closed, he eyed her hungrily. She was young, pretty, and trusting. Perfect for his wants. Perfect for his needs.

There was a small cooler nestled between the passenger and driver's seats. He opened it up to reveal it was full of halfway melted ice and two repurposed Gatorade bottles now filled with ice water. He offered one to Amanda. "Thirsty?"

"Oh, yes, thank you." She gladly took it and unscrewed the top. She wiped down the lip of the bottle with her sleeve before greedily downing the cold water. Once finished, she let out a satisfied sigh.

Frank eyed her as she drank. "There's some flavoring packets in the glove box if you'd like. I think there's cherry and watermelon."

"That's alright." Amanda said. "Just the water's fine with me."

It was nearly full dark when they got to town. Frank pulled his truck into a gas station and started to fill it up. "So," he said, "what are you going to do now?"

"See if I can get a tow truck for my car. If that doesn't work, then I'll have to try calling my parents, see if I can get a hold of someone and get a ride home." She pulled her phone from her bag. "Thanks again for the ride. It was really kind of you."

"Don't mention it." Frank said.

She quickly dialed a number and moved out of earshot. This wasn't working the way he wanted. If she contacted someone, then he'd miss his chance.

She was pretty, a sweet little thing to be around, and naive. A perfect girl for him, but that opportunity was slipping away. He needed to do something soon if he wanted to keep her.

"I don't believe this," Amanda said as she came back to the truck. "My battery died in the middle of my call." She threw it back into her bag with frustration. "That's just perfect!"

"Wow, what bad luck." Frank was laughing inside. No way for her to call for help, no one to come get her. "What now?"

Amanda ran a hand through her hair. "I guess I'll need to find a motel or something around here. Charge my phone, get some sleep, and try again in the morning. I don't suppose you know where one is, do you?"

This was too perfect an opportunity. "I'm actually heading to one right now." He hadn't been planning on it before, but now he was. "I'd be willing to share a room and split the difference if you'd like. It'd be less expensive that way."

"Oh, that would be so nice of you, but I really can't," Amanda said. "You've been so generous already, I shouldn't impose."

"Don't worry about it." The truck finished gassing up and he returned to nozzle to its place. Now, things were working out better for him than he could have expected. It was almost too good to be true. What was he going to do to her first? Drug her? Tie her down and tear her clothes off? Maybe use her panties as a gag while having his way with her? The thoughts were making him hard just thinking about it. "Come on, hop in." He said as he got back into the truck.

The motel was a run down place often used for short secret rendezvous and liaisons. It still used regular metal keys instead of cards for the doors.

They checked in together, were given their key, and once in the room found it had only one bed. "Oh, I guess I forgot to specify a two bed room," Frank said as they walked in. "It's okay, I'll take the floor. You can have the bed."

"That's very nice of you." Amanda stated. She brushed the hair out of her face and closed the door behind her. She sighed. "I'm dying for a shower. Excuse me." She stepped past Frank and let herself into the bathroom. The door locked behind her.

The sound of running water filled the small

motel room. Steam wafted out from under the door. Frank lay himself across the bed and turned the TV on. He wasn't watching anything in particular, just killing time until she came out. Once her shower was done, then he would have his fun.

The shower soon came to a stop, followed by the sound of the running sink and teeth brushing. Interesting that the girl had her toothbrush with her, but whatever. Once the brushing stopped, the door unlocked and Amanda stepped out.

Frank was shocked to see her with only a towel wrapped around her wet, naked body. He assumed she would get dressed before exiting the bathroom, but there she stood in the doorway, one hand clasping the towel at her breasts with the other arm propped against the wall. The towel's edges parted slightly to reveal a long patch of bare skin which ran from her upper thigh up to her chest.

Amanda stared at him, a perky smile across her lips and eyes giving a sultry look. "I was thinking," she said as she stepped out from the doorway, "I didn't quite know how to repay you for all you've done for me today." She stood between him and the TV, swaying slightly to one side and then the other.

Her hands went to the towel's corners and slow pulled them apart, just enough to show some skin and nothing else. "And then it just hit me, the most obvious way to show my appreciation." The towel fell to the floor by her feet.

Frank could not believe this turn of events. This beautiful twenty-something girl, wet and naked, and now crawling on the bed towards him. It was almost too easy. All right, he could go for this. The first time can be consensual, it'd been a long time since the last encounter like that, but after this it would be on his terms.

Amanda straddled him, her hands going for his belt and zipper. As she leaned in close, Frank noticed the faint whiff of perfume in the air and the bright red lipstick she wore. Had she been planning this the whole time? Maybe she was one of those big city whores. Oh, well. Now wasn't the time for thinking. But if she expected to get paid, she was dead wrong. And once he was done with her, she'd be just plain dead.

He placed his hands on her breasts, caressing them. They kissed, tongues sliding together. Her lips were soft and moist.

Suddenly, his body felt tingly and ridged, and not in the good way. Frank's eyes snapped open and he pulled away. His mouth had a strange prickly feeling to it, like he'd been shot full of Novocain. He tried to push her off, but his arms lost their strength. He collapsed back to the bed, unable to move his body. His heart raced, breathing became difficult.

Amanda smirked. She climbed off the bed and moved across the room back to her travel bag. "Feeling strange? I'd expect so. As you might have guess, there's a poison in the lipstick."

Poison lipstick? She must've put some kind of paralyzing agent in it. So, she had been planning this since the beginning, but nothing in the way that he thought. He struggled to move, but his body would not respond.

"Don't bother. You'll be like that for hours. Of course, I took the antidote while in the bathroom. Don't worry, I brushed my teeth and rinsed out my mouth, just to make sure you didn't catch any little traces." Amanda came back to the bed, a stretch of nylon rope in her hands. "You men are all the same. You see a pretty girl and can't help but give her a hand. You make such easy targets." She climbed on top of him and coiled the rope around his neck. "Don't worry. It'll all be over soon."

She gave a quick jerk on the rope, cutting off his windpipe. Frank struggled, he sputtered for breath, but still his body didn't move. His lungs burned for air, fingers twitched as he fought to move, and eyes clouded over. He coughed and gagged, but could not escape. Finally, his tremors stopped, and he fell limp on the bed.

* * *

The woman brought the pick-up truck to a halt in the middle of an old bridge. Below, a mountain river crashed and burst against the jutting rocks in its path.

She stepped out of the cab and walked around to the pick-up bed. Inside was a large black weather tarp wrapped around the body of her latest victim, a pair of cinder blocks tied to the feet.

After she'd killed him, she made quick work emptying his bank account of every penny, along with pawning whatever valuables he'd had. It wasn't worth a lot, he wasn't one of the usual targets she goes after. This was just a quick buck.

She dragged the body over to the edge of the bridge, and then with a strong kick, sent it careening to the river below. A spray of water shot into the air before the corpse disappeared into the dark waters. Satisfied with herself, Amanda climbed back into her new stolen truck and drove away.

The body sank down to the rocky riverbed. It struck the bottom, landing right next to the already decaying corpse of the man's previous victim.

Wingbeats in the Night

Chapter 1: The Pyramid

There are those who ask why I fear to venture out after dark. Why the sight of the setting sun fills me with dread, and the sounds of beating wings is enough to incite pure white panic. I assure you, it wasn't always so.

There was once a time when I would take long, leisure walks in the dead of night when the world was asleep. Those days are behind me now, and by the end of my tale, you'll understand why.

The cause of my phobia occurred two years ago when I took a vacation to Mexico to visit ancient sites of Aztec and Mayan ruins. My fascination with primitive, ancient cultures stretched all the way back to my earliest years when I was first introduced to the wonders of Egypt and the Pharaohs. As I grew older, my interests expanded beyond Egypt to included Greece and Rome, along with the cultures of Mesopotamia, China, Japan, India, and Tibet. My local librarians knew me by name, attesting to the countless hours I spent in their halls, browsing their collections of ancient civilizations and devouring book after book, my mind absorbing what I read like a sponge.

I longed one day to visit some of these amazing sites and visit these ruins for myself. Being that I lacked sufficient funds, traveling across the globe would be exceedingly difficult. However, I appreciated not just the cultures of the old world, but those of the Americas as well. Specifically, the great monuments and pyramids of Central and South America. So when I became old enough, and amassed enough of a fortune to travel, I planned a trip to visit the ancient city of the Sun Pyramid.

Once in Mexico City, I sought a local guide to take me. I wanted to not be seen as just another ignorant American tourist with their Bermuda shorts, socks and sandals, tacky shirt, and sunscreen-covered nose, with a camera dangling around my neck. I wished to experience the ancient city for myself, more authentically than was possible with an agency in a large crowd. To that end, I asked the receptionist at my hotel as I checked in, and was recommended a man named

Javier Romero.

"*Señor* Romero is the man you want," the receptionist told me. "He spends many a summer venturing into the jungle, taking rich adventurers and thrill seekers. He knows where many lost shrines and temples reside, even a lost pyramid. If you want a true experience, he's who you call."

The receptionist took one of the hotel cards and scrawled a number on the back, then handed it to me. Once in my room, I called the number and was immediately connected with this Javier Romero.

After I explained what I wanted, he said. "*Si, señor.* I won't take you to Sun Pyramid. Too many tourists, too many crowds. Full of pickpockets and con artists. No, I know a better place. An unknown temple deep in the jungle and away from all people.

You got the money, I get us the ride. This pyramid is unlike any other in the world. We go *mañana*. I get you at your hotel in the morning. *Comprende?*"

I understood, but I had some suspicions. I knew some pretty terrible things could happen to unwary tourists in Mexico. Someone might go down the wrong street or talk to the wrong person, and never be seen again or their picture would be featured on a collage of missing persons posters. All these things crossed my mind as I lay in my hotel bed, thinking on the journey.

Despite how I tried, I couldn't get to sleep. With nothing else to do, I opened up my bag and took out my pocket directory on the myths and legends of the Aztecs and Mayans. I clicked on my bedside lamp and opened the book.

The first deity I came upon was that of the bat god of the underworld, *Camazotz*. I'd seen this page before, and was familiar with the being it presented, a human-bat hybrid that fed on the flesh and blood of its victims. It had the wings and face of a bat, and the body shape of a man. According to the book, the Mayans used to offer human sacrifices to this god, tens of thousands a year across their empire.

How naive I was back then. Had I known what was to follow, I'd have returned home that night, regardless of the money spent. Even now, just remembering the picture on the page gives me chills.

I slept very little that night. In the morning, after eating a complimentary breakfast provided by the hotel, I ventured outside to wait. After several minutes, an old, clunking, rickety white pickup truck pulled alongside me. The engine shut off in a metal-grinding rattle, the door creaked open, and a middle-aged Mexican man stepped out.

His white shirt was stained with dirt and dust, and his faded blue jeans were ripped at both knees, as well as a half-dozen other places. His hair was a mix of black and gray, and it fell past his shoulders.

"*Hola*," he said with a wave of his hand. "Are you my *viajero*?"

I had to think back on my limited Spanish, but soon remembered *viajero* meant *traveler*. "Yes, sir," I said, then caught myself. "Um . . . *si, señor.*"

"*Si, hola*," he said again, shaking my hand and clapping me on the shoulder. "I am Javier Romero.

Come," he motioned me to the truck, took my suitcase and tossed it in the bed of the truck beside his own duffle bag. "We must hurry before the sun sets."

"Sunset?" I checked my phone. It was only a few minutes past ten. The sun was high and warm with plenty of daylight left.

"*Si*. Is a long drive to get there." He opened the truck's passenger door which creaked on rusty old hinges. "*Entra*," he said.

I did as asked, and we headed off. The truck's engine seemed to be a constant grind of metal and gears, and part of me wondered when it had last been maintained.

We drove for hours. It wasn't long before we left the city behind and found ourselves on a long, open highway deserted of all other signs of modern civilization. The foliage grew thicker along the roadside the further we drove. It soon turned from simple dense vegetation into true jungle. After a while, we left the highway behind as well.

We turned onto a smaller road, and then onto a smaller road still. The further we went, the less maintained the road became until there was no pavement at all, just warn, hard packed dirt. By mid afternoon, the trees cleared for the briefest moment and I saw between them, rising up out of the jungle, the very top of a stone step pyramid.

Several minutes later, we reached the pyramid itself. A massive stone monument, archaic and ageless, towering over the jungle canopy. Its sides were not sloped like those from Egypt, but rather a series of ever decreasing platforms built atop one another until they reached the ceremonial sacrificial platform on the structure's pinnacle.

My guide gathered his duffle bag from the bed of the truck and we ascended the pyramid together. The steps were sloped downward, so the heel of my foot fell lower than my toes, making the climb much more difficult. However, my guide seemed unbothered by this, as his last steps at the top were just as powerful as his first.

Along either side of the staircase, carved images of ancient Mesoamerican deities were etched in stone. The most prominent at the start was the feathered serpent *Kukulcan,* or Quetzalcoatl. As we climbed closer to the summit, the carvings changed. Fewer feathered serpents appeared, and more often the creatures depicted had large membranous wings, tall pointed ears, wide bulging eyes, and prominent pointed fangs.

About halfway up, Javier pulled from the duffle bag a pop top water bottle. He opened the nozzle, but instead of drinking, he sprayed himself in the face with water. Before putting it away, he offered it to me. "You want?" He asked. "Don't worry, my friend," He poured some water in his cupped hand and drank. "Is clean. Filtered. Safe."

I would've refused had he not drank some himself. In retrospect, I should have declined anyways. As it was, I found my throat parched and my face warm, so I accepted his offer. Meaning to only take a small sip, I instead found myself downing nearly half the bottle at once. I tried to apologize when I handed it back to him, but Javier seemed not to mind. He simply closed the bottle, tucked it back in his duffle, then continued up the steep staircase.

It was late afternoon, bordering on evening, when we reached the very peak of the pyramid. Once there, Javier reached into his duffle and pulled out two cave-diving hardhats with light bulb fixtures attached to the front, and handed one to me.

"Wear this," he said. "It will be dark inside." I did as he directed, checking the light to make sure it worked. Once we confirmed it did, we entered the upmost temple at the top of the pyramid.

Inside, in the center of the main chamber, was a stone table or altar shaped like a reclining man. The surface was rough and pitted, as though something corrosive had been poured on it.

It was also stained with old blood. At where the stone man's chest would be, red streaks radiated outward, spilling down the sides and even marking the floor.

"This," Javier said as he came to stand beside me, "was where they offered human sacrifices to their gods." He stepped around the altar, keeping his headlight fixed on the blood-stained surface. "The offering would lay here, sometimes with priests holding their arms and legs, while the High Priest preformed the ceremony."

Already I could feel my heart racing. Staring at the altar, noticing how worn and rough the stone was, I also saw how vibrant the red color stood out against it. I could even smell the metallic scent of the blood, and that realization frightened me as well. This altar looked freshly used. But that should be impossible. The Mayan civilization had been extinct for hundreds of years before the Conquistadors landed in Mexico. Even if the Aztec had used it afterwards, that practice would have ended over five hundred years ago. But this blood looked to be a few weeks old at most. Maybe more recent even than that.

"The sacrifice's heart was cut from their chest while they still lived," my guide continued. While I had known this from a scholarly point of view, gazing upon one of the sights where it happened brought another, stronger feeling of dread over me. I didn't want to think of it, but my mind's eye conjured the image without my consent.

A man forced on the stone altar, each of his limbs held down by a priest's assistants. The man would struggle, he would fight against those holding him, but they were too strong and too many. His efforts proved in vain.

Then the High Priest himself would appear; his head adorned with a tall headdress made of bright green and blue feathers of jungle birds, a jaguar skin cloak draped along his back, gold and jade earrings and bracelets. In his hand, the High Priest held a black obsidian knife that glistened in the light of dancing flames.

At the sight of the knife, the victim would struggle anew. He'd scream for mercy, beg for his life, but nothing could deter his killers.

The High Priest would begin chanting a prayer, the words also taken up by the assistants holding the victim's limbs. Then he would raise the black obsidian blade over his head, and plunge it deep into the sacrifice's chest.

In my mind, I witnessed it all. I saw the spurt of blood as the knife struck. I heard the man's scream change into a gasping, choking gurgle. I even saw the shadows on the wall as the High Priest reached into the man's open rib cage and lifted out his still beating heart. Somehow, in all of this, the face of the High Priest changed to mirror that of my guide, Javier Romero.

I clenched my eyes shut and turned away from the bloody altar. I bit my lip and held my breath for several long seconds, then finally allowed myself to open my eyes again. To distract my overworked mind, I moved to examine the rest of the main chamber.

Across the back wall, directly behind the sacrificial altar, an etching was carved into the rock. It depicted some kind of rite or ceremony, an offering to their gods. The image engraved in stone was the very reflection of what I'd imagined; a man held down by his arms and legs across a sacrificial altar, his chest cut open, and his heart held towards the sky in the hands of a priest.

All of this, however, merely represented the bottom half of the carving. The top half, looming larger than all the rest, was the image of an enormous part-man, part-bat monstrosity.

"This temple was dedicated to his worship,"

Javier said, shinning his light on the carved mural. "Lord of the dead, god of the Underworld. The death bat, *Camazotz*."

My heart beat even harder now. I could feel it thundering in my chest at an unusual pace. My whole body felt warm. I reached up to wipe sweat from my brow, but when I raised my hand I saw it shake and tremble before me. My chest felt heavy, and I struggled to take a breath. My vision started to blur. From the growing distance of my surroundings, I could still hear Javier speak.

"At night, *Camazotz* and his legions would rise from *Xibalba*, out of the caves beneath these temples to devour the hearts of those offered to them." He set his duffle bag on the floor and unzipped. "Tonight is one such night."

My legs grew weak, and I found I could barely stand. I stumbled backwards, grasping hold of the sacrificial altar for support. My arms and legs grew numb, like ghost limbs. As Javier removed the water bottle from his bag I realized what must've happened. The water was drugged! I was succumbing to the effects of whatever he'd laced it with.

I tried to run, but my uncoordinated legs tangled among themselves. I lurched forward, my useless arms flailing impotently at my sides, and collapsed with all the grace of a felled tree. My head hit the stone floor, and I was engulfed in darkness.

Chapter 2: The Ritual

I don't know whether to be grateful or not that this isn't the end of my story. Sometimes, I wish it was. If I had not awakened some hours later, I would not have seen what I've seen. I would not know what I now know.

But I did awaken. I awoke to the sounds of beating drums, and the smell of smoke. At first it was a distant, rhythmic thumping in the dark. The beating steadily grew louder and closer until I opened my eyes.

I was still in the main chamber of the pyramid. I was on my back, staring up through the open ceiling at the full moon overhead. The inner chamber was lit by the dancing flames of a wall-mounted torch behind me, which cast shifting shadows along the walls. The air was thick with the wafting scent of smoke.

I tried to move, and found myself tied down. A rope coiled around my body, my arms and legs bound tight. My shirt was gone. I spotted it tossed in a corner on the floor. Beside it lay Javier's now empty duffle bag.

In the very back of the chamber, sitting in front of the carved depiction of the bat god, Javier sat cross-legged on the floor. In his lap he was beating an animal-skin drum. His face was covered with black and red paint, crossing back and forth across his skin in a grotesque mockery of a bat's face. He wore a headdress of blue and green feathers on his head, and a jaguar-skin cloak on his back.

On the floor to his left, right beside his foot, lay a black blade that glistening like glass. An obsidian knife.

"Oh, God," I said at once. I shut my eyes and turned away. "This can't be happening. Dear God, this can't be happening." Warm, wet tears spilled from my eyes. "Please, let this be a dream! Just a dream!"

The drumming continued uninterrupted. "This is no dream," Javier said. "And your god cannot help you. This is the domain of another, one that's been here far longer than your Christian god."

A chirping, squeaking noise come from outside. I opened my eyes and looked through the open ceiling again at the silver-white disk of the full moon. In that moment, a small black shadow passed in front of the moon, followed shortly by another. And yet another.

Soon, a whole swarm of these small creatures appeared. They flew in a great spiraling column upwards towards the cloudless sky, the flutter of their wings and their continuous chirping squeaks deafened all other sounds, save the beating of Javier's drum, to oblivion.

The drumming stopped as Javier retrieved the knife and rose to his feet. Javier stood over me, the black obsidian blade glistened in the dancing torchlight. He raised it, and in that instant I knew what he would do. He was going to plunge the blade into my chest and rip my heart out, holding it up for me to see in the brief moments before my death.

But he didn't. He slid the edge across his open palm, coating his own hand in blood, then pressed his bloody hand against my chest. "You are marked," he said. "And soon, your essence will go to feed the great *Camazotz*." He pulled his hand away, leaving a red print across my chest. He then set the knife on the floor beside the pedestal, returned to his drum, and began beating it again while chanting in a bizarre tongue I can only assume was ancient Mayan.

Looking down at my chest, I could see the bloody handprint he'd marked me with. Even now, with the warmth of his blood rapidly cooling, some part of me still insisted this was nothing by a horrible nightmare.

"It is a great honor," Javier said. "Your heart, your soul, will be fed to the great beings of old. In the ancient times, when our numbers were great, we would offer thousands of sacrifices to the gods a year. Now, we are too few. They grow anxious and hungry. But while our numbers may dwindle, we will never be destroyed.

"The Spanish tried and failed. The English, the Americans, even the Mexican government has tried. All have failed. And someday, when the stars are right, *Camazotz* will rise from *Xibalba* with his legions of the dead to conquer the living world. Until that day, we, his loyal servants, will offer blood as sustenance. So don't be afraid. Your death serves a higher purpose."

I redoubled my struggles, but still the rope held me. It bit into my sides, my arms, and my chest each time I tugged against it. It was then I noticed how old and worn the rope was. It was stained not just with dirt and grime, but blood as well. How many times had this very rope been used to secure someone to this same altar, I cannot say.

The fibers had frayed in places. Most was normal wear and tear, but there was one section that looked as though it had nearly been severed through. Perhaps the knife had slipped and nicked the rope when . . . when . . . when it was being used.

In any case, that frayed section of rope was my only chance of escape. I shifted my body as best I could until that piece of rope rubbed against the corner of the stone altar. I began moving my arm and shoulder back and forth, scrapping the damaged rope against the rock. Steadily, the fibers started to weaken.

The flapping of wings and chattering of bats outside grew louder as they swarmed. Looking through the skylight in the ceiling, I noticed how the swarm circled directly over the pyramid.

Just then, a new silhouette appeared amongst the others; one much larger than the rest. As it passed in front of the moon, the silver disk's light was completely obscured by the beast's enormous leathery wings.

"He is here," Javier said, his head craned back and his eyes staring out the hole in the ceiling. A smile of pure delight spread across his face. He clamored to his feet and raised both hands into the air, shouting and chanting his ancient, dead language in reverence to his heinous god.

Something landed on the outside of the pyramid. The moon was directly behind it, so all I saw was its vague black outline, but that was enough to fuel my nightmares for as long as I live. It was the size of a man, but crouched and coiled like a beast. Hair bristled along its back, like small porcupine quills. Its wings, membranous and leathery, extended for nearly five feet both to its left and right.

A normal bat would have a single opposable thumb on each wing, but this creature had three independent digits; I saw them as it crouched over the skylight and its clawed fingers coiled around the lip of the open ceiling.

Its face hovered just out of range of the torchlight, but I saw enough. Two ears, tall and pointed like devil horns atop the creature's head. Its lips pulled back and I saw the glistening shimmer of firelight across rows of sharp teeth. And the eyes, two points of shining red light in that dark mask of a face. Red eyes fixated on me.

Javier approached me again. He retrieved the obsidian knife and clutched it in both hands with the blade point down at the bloody handprint on my chest.

My eyes felt as though they would bulge out of my head. My breath came in rapid, shallow bursts I couldn't control. Even with him standing over me, I scraped the thin section of rope faster against the rough stone.

He never stopped chanting; his lips moved constantly, and the string of ancient Mayan words flowed like a cursed waterfall from his mouth. I saw his eyelids flutter as his eyes rolled back. He raised the ceremonial dagger over his head.

There was a snap, almost like the bang from a starter's gun, and the binds around me loosened. I'd managed to saw through the damaged rope. Without thinking, I shoved myself off the altar just as Javier brought down the knife. The tip of the dagger struck the stone altar and I heard a cracking behind me as the obsidian blade shattered on impact.

I scrambled to my feet, my heart pounding with such force I feared I might faint even then. I raced out of the sacrificial chamber, glancing back for only the briefest of moments to see Javier leaping over the altar in pursuit.

Once outside, the constant chirping and clicking of the bats, along with the beating of their wings, assaulted my ears. I ran for the steps and I took them two, even three at a time. Never mind that I was running blind down the pyramid's steep slope, the only light being the untrustworthy silver glow of the moon. That I also did not know where I was running to did not concern me. Just that I had to get out, had to get away.

That deceiving moonlight dimmed, and I heard an earsplitting shriek. The large shadow rose overhead, a massive field of darkness that could've been torn straight from the night itself. I glanced back for only a moment, enough to see the demonic monstrosity rise into the air, surrounded by the spiraling swarm of bats against the moon.

And right on my heels, Javier pursuing me. He lunged for me, his muscular arms wrapped around my midsection, pitching me forward.

Whether it was conscious on my part or pure happenstance, I will never know. When he struck me, my right foot slipped and I twisted to one side. We fell together and crashed against the stone steps, myself on top and Javier beneath me. There was a sickening, teeth-rattling crunch as Javier's bones shattered.

His body had cushioned my fall and protected me from any major injury. I wasted no time. Still flushed with adrenaline, I was on my feet and running almost before I realized what happened.

At the base of the pyramid sat the truck we'd driven in. I raced for it, my only hope of salvation. I couldn't even remember if the doors were locked or not. I could only hope.

I grasped the handle and pushed the chrome button. The door groaned in protest, but it opened with a rusty creak. I threw myself across the seats inside and yanked the door shut with a deafening slam.

The same moment the door closed, I heard a soft thump against the window. It was followed by another, along with the beating of wings and chattering click of bats. The thumping noise soon came from all sides as hundreds of bats knocked against the sides of the truck. But they couldn't get in. They were too small, too light.

I placed a hand against my chest, feeling the racing of my heart finally start to subside. In here, I was safe. They couldn't get me. I took a deep breath and let it out, then allowed my eyes to close.

There was a loud thunk and the truck jostled violently on its shocks as something large and heavy landed on the roof. My slowing heart rate skyrocketed once again, my eyes bulged, and I pressed myself against the seat. Looking out the windshield, I saw nothing except the perimeter of dense jungle all around, along with the passing swoops of the smaller bats. Overhead, the roof creaked and groaned as the creature shifted its weight from one side to the other, its sharp claws scraping against the metal.

A loud shriek echoed outside just as the weight lifted off the truck. The bats congregated into another spiraling column in the air, before descending over the fallen, broken, yet still moving body of Javier lying on the stone steps.

It was too much for me. I exhaled, fell back across the seats, and lost consciousness once again.

Chapter 3: The Sacrifice

I awoke the next morning to the hot jungle sun shining through the truck's windshield. I winced and turned away, sitting up so the light wasn't directly in my eyes. My head throbbed. My whole body was a mess of aches and pains. The inside of the truck's cab smelled of dried blood.

Looking outside, I saw no sign of the creatures from last night. The pyramid still stood tall and monolithic, a rough gray against the overwhelming green of the jungle around it.

Upon the stairs, less than halfway to the pyramid's summit, lay the dismembered, gnawed clean bones of my guide. Even from this distance, myself in the truck and his skeleton on the pyramid's steps, I could see his skull lying on its side, the empty sockets staring back at me. It appeared to be grinning.

My stomach lurched. I averted my gaze, my eyes clamped shut. Never before had I felt such a strong desire to leave a place. Looking at the steering wheel, I spotted the keys dangling from the ignition. Javier had never taken them out. Why would he? After all, there was no chance of someone stealing the truck.

I shifted over to the driver's side and twisted the key. The engine ground and choked, then rumbled to life. With one final haunted look back at the stone pyramid, I put the truck in gear and drove back along the barely marked jungle trail.

The roads grew better maintained the further I drove. From a simple trail, to a dirt road, until finally asphalt. The day was hot and humid. I tried to turn the air conditioning on, only to find the truck had none. I opened a window instead, grateful to get some air movement.

Inside, the cab still smelled of dried blood. Looking down, I found the source of that smell; the bloody handprint Javier had left across my chest. I licked my thumb and tried to rub part of it off, but the handprint wouldn't even smudge.

The needle on the gas gauge dipped low, dangerously close to empty well before I reached Mexico City. At the first gas station I saw, a single ramshackle shack and pump on the side of the road,

I pulled over. To deal with my shirtless state, I walked around to the bed of the truck where my suitcase still lay, somehow undisturbed in spite of the night's events. I opened it to find a new shirt for myself, as well as my wallet.

The first shirt I pulled out was a casual shirt with a floral print. I threw it on, neglecting to button it just yet, then grabbed my wallet and went to speak with the attendant. He was an older gentleman with a thick mustache, wearing a broad cowboy hat and boots. As he came out to see me, his eyes instantly fell on my chest.

"*Los santos nos salvan*," he muttered, crossing himself.

"What? I'm sorry, I don't understand."

"You are marked, *señor*," the old man said,

pointing to the bloody handprint. "*El Diablo* will come for you soon. There is no escape. You must leave now."

"I can't. I need gas, the truck's empty."

"Take all you want. No charge. Just go, and never come back." He retreated inside his small store and shut the door behind him. He didn't reemerge again the whole time I was there.

Nearby, tacked on a corkboard next to the small store's front entrance, hung dozens of missing person posters. The faces displayed on those faded, sun-bleached papers were from all walks of life; some were of rich American tourists, others of poor rural Mexicans. The oldest was a seventy-five-year-old man, the youngest an eight-year-old girl. Men, women, children, all were included.

My thoughts turned to things Javier had said last night. How there were more like him, more followers and worshipers of the old gods, how they would never be destroyed, and how they would continue offering sacrifices until *Camazotz* rose to enslave the world of the living. I thought of those things as I looked across the faces of the missing.

The realization struck. Some, maybe even most of the missing people were the victims of cartels, drug-runners, and traffickers, but not all of them. How many were the unfortunate victims of a ritual far older and more sinister? How many had been in the same position as I, bound to an altar with a knife over their chest, and a legion of blood-thirsty demons swarming around them? Those poor souls who, unlike me, didn't escape.

I filled the truck as quick as I could, then drove away without another word. I rejected any previous notion I might have had of returning to the hotel; after all it was the receptionist who connected me with Javier. I had no doubt they were secret worshipers of *Camazotz* the same as him. And who else might be? How many more throughout the country might still be followers of that depraved faith? How many throughout the world?

I could not stay any longer. I needed to leave and get back to the States as soon as possible. I drove without stopping all the way back to the airport and changed my return flight to the first one I could book. It was an extra three hundred dollars, but I didn't care. The whole time I was in the airport, I received looks and stares from other passengers and travelers. Some were looks of concern, but I'm sure just as many were members of the *Camazotz* cult, eyeing me as the sacrifice that escaped his fate. For the time being at least.

Now I come to the end of my tale. I made it home safely, but I don't feel safe anymore. I fear I never will. The mark on my chest, that blood-stained handprint, has never washed off or even faded, no matter how much I scrub it or what cleaning products I use. Even bleach did nothing to lessen its image or its scent.

The worst comes at night. I never noticed them before, but now I can't ignore it. The constant chattering and flapping of leather wings whenever I step foot outside after sunset.

I don't know exactly what I saw that night. It

might've just been some enormous species of bat hitherto unknown to science. Perhaps it was *Camazotz* himself, come to claim the human sacrifice offered to him. It might not have been *Camazotz* at all, merely a servant of his acting on the death god's behalf.

Whatever the case may be, I fear I'm not long for this world. The old man at the gas station was right; I am marked. The cult of *Camazotz* lives. They will come for me someday. Until that moment comes, I will constantly be haunted by the unending torments of their denizens, the winged beasts that fly in the dark. Unable to escape the sound of those flying hell spawn, those servants of evil, the wingbeats in the night.

Other Books by N. J. Hanson:

Stand Alone Works:

The Last Stand of the Dragon

Frost Bite: Cannibal in the Forest

The Ravenwood Hauntings:

An Empty Swing

The Broken Chain

The Kingdom of Dadria:

A Lamb Amongst Wolves

The Blood of Wolves and War

Co-authored with Hope Hill:

Secrets Under the Skin